Frogs and

the *Ballet*

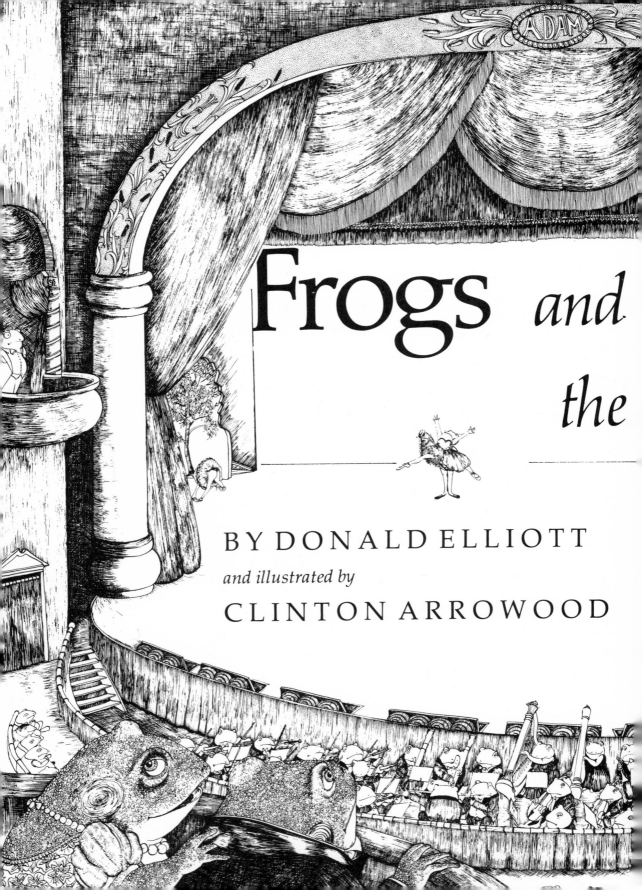

Frogs and the

BY DONALD ELLIOTT

and illustrated by

CLINTON ARROWOOD

Ballet

1 9 7 9

Published by G A M B I T

of Meeting House Green in Ipswich

MASSACHUSETTS

First Printing

Library of Congress Cataloging in Publication Data

Elliott, Donald.
Frogs and the ballet.

SUMMARY: Introduces familiar ballet steps, demonstrating what lies behind these seemingly effortless movements and how they are woven into classical ballet.
1. Ballet dancing—Juvenile literature. [1. Ballet dancing] I. Arrowood, Clinton. II. Title.
GV1788.E54   792.8's   78-19566
ISBN 0-87645-099-0

Dedication

For Connie Thompson, whose gentle elegance and depth of feeling and understanding made her truly a 'première danseuse' in life's fleeting dance.

Contents

A Preface

This book is composed of several sections. To begin with, there is "A Serious Foreword," a fairly brief and somewhat ponderous introduction touching on some basic aspects of ballet.

Having disposed of the Foreword, which the reader may dispose of as he or she sees fit, we present you with a series of illustrations designed to whet your appetite for the ballet and, possibly, for the hitherto unsuspected elegance of the Family Ranidae, if you are not terribly familiar with either. If, however, one or both are subjects with which you do regularly keep in touch, we would like to offer another view of them to add to those you already have.

On the theory that a look, even a somewhat myopic one, at almost anything from a unique angle may be better than a clear-sighted gaze that never changes its focus or its perspective, we present you with a fairly singular view that will, we hope, illuminate or at least challenge your perception of the ballet.

Thanks are due to many who aided in the preparation of this book through their comments and reactions, particularly to Lovell Thompson of Gambit for his wisdom and unruffled tenacity, to Mrs. John Gibbon for her patience, tolerance and hospitality, to Vicki Nathanson for enlightening explanations, to Bess Cranley for valuable technical assistance, to Cielito Elliott for firm critical evaluation, and to Robinne Comissiona, who has spent much of her life immersed in the world of music and ballet and for whose kind and thoughtful willingness to help we are much indebted.

Last, and perhaps least, but not to be omitted, acknowledgment is due to Galatéa, Clinton Arrowhead's pet African frog, who served the artist with unrepining dedication throughout as his chief model for many members of the Corps-de-Frog-Ballet. Her imperturable passivity, her patient immobility and her vacantly steadfast gaze never wavered through many hours of modeling for her devoted owner.

A Serious Foreword

The Hierarchy of History

There is a very real sense in which nearly all attempts to acquire knowledge and understanding eventually reduce themselves to a process of categorization, to the development or discovery of an order of one sort or another. This is most certainly true in the areas of science and mathematics, where through the ages man has attempted to wrest from his experience and his imagination a conceptualized framework that would serve to lay open to his gaze the intricate but ordered workings of his universe. And there are ways in which his artistic impulse— itself an attempt to acquire and communicate some kind of insight and understanding—can also be considered to have resulted in creations that reflect a similar kind of hierarchical order.

There is considerable evidence, for example, that the human desire to express and to communicate feeling and understanding by means of rhythmic body movements is nearly as old as man himself, although its earliest manifestations must have been exceedingly primitive indeed. But the impulse was there, and the process of cultural evolution in this area is a history of any number of refined and highly distinctive sub-categories of that initial mighty, irresistible and well-nigh universal urge.

The classic ballet, in the idiom and style we know today and as theatrical production, is probably no more than about two centuries old, despite its foundations that lie in the wellsprings of humanity. Its origins and development were in Europe, and, somewhat later, in the United States, and its earliest forms were displayed in the courts of European royalty. Examined, refined, perfected, and endowed with a terminology that is French in origin, it has come to us today as a highly organized, highly stylized and exceedingly complex system of rhythmic movements that not only follows the line of intricate instrumental music but also usually tells a story. Ballet, then, is theatre, it is music, it is virtuoso dancing, and it is a unique form of artistic expression.

Ballet, from a purely logical point of view, is merely one very specific, very categorized example of an essential and broadly inclusive human creative force. But it lies amid all the products of that force like a highly faceted and polished diamond with all the perfection, harmony and beauty of that rarest and most valuable of gems.

Motion and Rhythm

Music and dance, unlike painting and sculpture, are art forms whose very essences lie in continuous movement and change. Meaning is inextricably bound up with variations within a pattern, and no single frozen glimpse can ever be sufficient to convey the intent of what is meant to be seen and heard over a period of time. Basic to the pattern is the existence of rhythm, the element that brings harmony and order to the flowing progression of sound and movement that is music and dance.

There is a way in which motion and, in particular, ordered motion, can be considered as being at the heart of the idea of existence itself. From the ancient Greek concept of the movements of heavenly bodies, the "Music of the Spheres," to that of the Renaissance, called by Jacob Bronowski "The Majestic Clockwork," there is the underlying notion of patterned movement. This concept has found its fullest development in the West, where the major thrust of virtually all art, literature, mathematics and science is concerned with process and search. The Greeks, well aware of the essential nature of patterns and movement, nonetheless placed their greatest emphasis on the nonmoving perfection of their temples and statuary and in the ethereal stillness of their unattainable worlds of absolute good, truth and beauty. It is the West, where the classic ballet has reached its highest development, that the imperfect in motion becomes more important than the perfect in repose, where an imperfect glimpse into the infinite carries more meaning than the attainment of a perfect moment.

The ballet, while it consists of an enormous number of body positions of great precision and rigid definition, is essentially an art or, even, science of movement. Consider, then, the difficulty, indeed the impossibility, of attempting to depict the ballet through a series of illustrations. The problem is akin to that of trying to show the movement of a breaking ocean wave with a single photograph. The depiction of a ballerina in a certain position, perhaps a foot or two off the floor with legs outstretched, toes pointed, arms extended, can show the graceful beauty of that position, but it can only suggest what went before and what will follow. The imagination must supply the rest, and, as with the wave, it is that exclusively human ability which allows a viewer to see movement in stillness and rhythmic pattern in the suspended moment.

Regardless of this difficulty, and the added one of the lack of any easily discernible organization of ballet positions and movements that would be susceptible to outlining and simplification, we have attempted to depict a few representative poses or steps that might be seen during a visit to a ballet production. Obviously, there is no substitute for attendance at a live performance, but perhaps our illustrations will, at least, present a view not normally seen at one.

The Sublime and the Ridiculous

The razor's edge between the sublime and the ridiculous is a boundary upon which so much and so many teeter precariously so often. Truth, overstated and projected beyond all endurance, dissolves into nonsense, and beauty, embellished and refined to the point of nausea, becomes a parody of itself. Kings, utterly bemused and unsettled by power and position, become asses, and philosophers, overwhelmed by their perspicacity, lose all touch with reality. The great joys of simplicity become lost in a welter of confusion, and art, intended to communicate with clarity and universality, lapses into confusion and irrelevancy.

One sees the prima donna in an opera, weighing 200 pounds, give or take a few, hiding demurely from her frantic lover who can't find her because she is concealed behind a spindly papier-mâché tree. Or one sees a ballet in which a grown man dashes madly across a stage and leaps vigorously and repeatedly into the air while beating his feet together. He is dressed in a costume which should be at least mildly embarrassing to anyone in his right mind but which, incredibly, raises only a very few eyebrows. The ballerina, standing on her *toes*, for the love of God, minces across the stage in tiny sidewise steps and then, suddenly descending to the soles of her feet, squats with her feet pointing in diametrically opposite directions. The audience murmurs in appreciation, and one wonders uneasily just how secure one's grip on reality truly is.

Now we ask you: how can one keep a clear view of that razor's edge, how can one retain at least a moderate grasp of his perspective on the sublime and the ridiculous? The question is not frivolous, for it is probably important to notice the emperor's new clothes and to be able to tell when he has them on and when he is just in his skivvies, or worse. In almost any area, particularly in the performing arts, and most especially in the ballet, the line is incredibly finely drawn. In most human endeavors a certain degree of incompetence is tolerable, perhaps even enhancing, since errors, within limits, sometimes have a way of inducing a kind of approval for one who is trying very hard and isn't quite perfect. But in the ballet anything much less than perfection comes perilously close to absurdity. One looks, then, for something very close to perfection; and since such a quest is in our humanly defective world so seldom rewarded, when true excellence is encountered, it is almost a sin to let it slip by unnoticed. And a sin of this sort is serious, for in the midst of so many of our ridiculous attempts at being serious it involves the possibility of missing a genuine glimpse of something in man which is the divine spark in him, which gives sense to the idea that he has been created in God's image. To see oneself as miserable and inconsequential in the light of immensity and eternity, but to see, too, that there is in a very real sense nothing that is more important than man, is to begin to have that perspective which enlightens and ennobles.

What, then, should one do in order to see in the ballet a bit of the deep meaning it can hold? Well, fortunately, nothing terribly intellectual is required; it is all more of an attitudinal sort of thing, of a kind of open approach which can allow feeling, removed from the fetters of analytical rationality, to respond to a view of controlled grace, of a blending of the physical and the spiritual, of an expression of beauty through a total union of mind, body and soul. All art may be considered as a magnificent attempt on our parts to communicate to one another our deplorably small understanding of ourselves and of our relationships to the endless concentric circles within which we live, and the only really successful art, then, is that in which that communication is not only given but also received.

We are serious, we are absurd; life is an earnest and

sober sort of thing and it is a trivial and giddy strut across a stage; art is sublime and it is ridiculous. But the person who sees one side without the other lives only half a life, and it is perhaps our great good fortune that the two sides are not really the opposite sides of a coin. They are very close to each other, they complement each other, and it is a bit comforting to think that God, while He is about managing His great serious plan of creation, is probably given to a good deal of mirth about the whole blessed situation.

The Anatomy of Ballet

Successful art is nearly always a combination of technique and artistic sensitivity, a fusion of a solid and competent grasp of the *means* of expression with the essential gift of having something to express. Technique alone is merely a kind of sterile skillfulness; artistic sensitivity or feeling alone, a frustrated glimpse of truth or beauty with no means of communication. They must exist together, one complementing the other, and when that occurs, great art is possible.

The technical demands imposed upon any artist are great indeed, but it is probable that no art requires as extensive and all-encompassing a grasp of technique as does ballet. In addition to possessing a flawless sense of rhythm and an enlightened understanding of music and of drama, the ballet dancer must meet the awesome and even horrendous challenges imposed by the physical demands of his or her art. The body must be able to accomplish what is unnatural and make it appear natural and almost effortless. The result, while a joy to behold, is a physical strain sufficient not infrequently to break bones, snap tendons and tear muscles. Practice for the dancer, whether as a beginner or as an accomplished artist, is incessant and unavoidable, and, while inactivity rapidly diminishes technical facility, the dancer must always live with the inescapable and bitter realization that the battle to stay in top form will always, in time, be lost.

Much of a ballet dancer's practice time, particularly at the beginning of a practice session, is spent at the *barre*, i.e., with the support of a kind of horizontal railing at or slightly above waist height. Basic movements that stretch the muscles and limber up the entire body are performed with the *barre* as an aid in maintaining balance. After this, in center practice, the dancer performs the same movements without the aid of the *barre*, relying on the entire body and especially on the positions of the hands and arms—known as *port de bras*—for the preservation of balance. Following this come the slow sustained movements, including turns or *pirouettes*, known as *adagio*, and only then does the dancer practice the big jumps, the *allegro*, and the beating together of the legs in midair, known as *batterie*. It is usually only at this stage that a female dancer will perform many of the previous positions and movements on full *pointes*, i.e., on the extreme tips of the toes.

While there is no simple categorization of ballet steps that would allow the uninitiated to grasp the vast gamut of movements comprising the ballet dancer's repertoire, there are some rather general divisions that can be made. It should be borne in mind that almost any step is subject to many variations. For example, a particular step that calls for, say, the left foot to move away from the right, may include variations in the direction of that step—forward, backward, to the side—and may also involve a number of alternative positions of the head, shoulders and arms. Thus, a truly formidable tome would be required to describe, even briefly, every possible step or movement that may be seen in an actual ballet performance.

Nevertheless, here are a few rather basic categorizations that might be made:

1. The five basic positions: These are the positions from which all or nearly all ballet movements begin and

in which they terminate. Many movements are subject to variations that depend on which of these positions is used as a beginning or an ending.

2. Movements at the *barre:* These comprise movements such as:

   a. *Demi-plié* or *grand plié*—a partial or full bending of the knees.

   b. *Battement*—literally, a "beating movement," in which one leg moves away from the other and then is returned to its original position, again, subject to a large number of variations.

   c. *Rond de jambe*—a circling motion of the leg.

   d. *Relevé*—a rising up on the toes, either to a *demi-pointe* position, on the balls of the feet, or to a full *pointe*, on the tips of the toes.

3. Movements at the center:

   a. *Temps lié*—a coordinated movement of arms and legs with a sliding motion of the foot.

   b. *Port de bras*—literally, "carriage of the arms," involving the position and movement of the arms and legs; the number and precise *attitudes* of these positions vary depending on different schools of ballet.

   c. *Épaulement*—literally, "carriage of the shoulders," involving the position and movement of the shoulders in relation to the head and arms, to the front or to either side.

   d. *Attitudes*—standing positions, of which there are a great number of variations.

   e. *Arabesques*—stances on one leg with the other raised behind, again with numerous variations.

   f. *Fouetté*—a movement involving a whipping motion of the legs.

   g. *Grand rond de jambe*—a movement involving a large

circling motion of the leg, executed with a jump or on *pointe*.

h. *Pirouettes and turning movements*—movements involving a complete turning of the body, once more with a great number of possible variations.

i. *Linking steps and movements*—such as *pas de bourrée, coupé, glissade* and *pas failli,* all of which are movements from one spot to another involving a transference of weight from one foot to the other.

4. Allegro: These movements consist to a large extent of jumping steps done in quick time, as opposed to the *adagio* movements, which are in slow time. They involve many of the steps performed at the *barre* and in the center, but in addition include *jetés*—jumps, and *batterie*—jumps with the legs, specifically the calves of the legs, brought together one or more times in the air. Probably the greatest number of individually designated movements are in these two areas, and we will here merely list some of them, forbearing any specific descriptions. Among the *jetés*, then, are the *temps levé, petit changement de pieds, petit echappé, grand echappé, pas assemblé, pas jeté, grand jeté, jeté fermé, jetés* by half turns, *jeté passé, jeté en tournant, sissonne ouverte, sissonne fermée, sissonne tombée, temps de cuisse, soubresaut, sissonne soubresaut, rond de jambe sauté, pas de chat, pas de basque, grand saut de basque, pas de ciseaux, pas ballotté, pas ballonné, pas chassé, emboîté en tournant, pas emboîté, pas balancé,* and—as if this were insufficient—numerous variations of all of these. Among the *batterie* are the *royale, entrechat, brisé fermé, cabriole,* and, of course, variations upon variations of these.

5. Dance on pointes: Dancing on *pointes*, that is, on the tips of the toes, is, in many ways, the ultimate achieve-

ment of the ballerina. Almost all the movements mentioned above can be performed on *pointes*, and the trained ballerina practices them—as well as the more fundamental exercises—in this manner, both at the *barre* and in the center. Specific movements often practiced on *pointes* include the *temps levé, échappé, glissade, temps lié; assemblié soutenu, jeté on pointes, sissonne simple* and *sissonne ouverte*.

6. Pas de deux: The term *pas de deux* refers to a dance designed specifically for duet performance. Although not restricted to the dancing of a ballerina with a male partner, this is its most usual form, and it is as such that we will treat it here. In earlier days, the function of the male dancer in a *pas de deux* was primarily, if not nearly exclusively, that of lending a literal physical support for the ballerina in many of her more spectacular movements, particularly in the *jetés*. As the ballet developed, however, the importance and individuality of the male dancer increased substantially, and today, while he still plays his supportive role, his dancing is often of a significance equivalent to that of his partner.

The physical support that the male dancer gives to the ballerina allows her, with his help, to leap farther, to lengthen the time in which she is actually in the air, to sustain certain positions, and to perform many movements that would be impossible alone. Many of the movements described above can also be performed as parts of a *pas de deux,* such as the *grand jeté, attitude* and *pirouette,* but some, for obvious reasons, are performed only as *pas de deux,* such as the *pas poisson, arabesque penchée* and various forms of shoulder lifts.

Now we are ready to show you illustrations of just a few

of the positions and movements that we have mentioned. The reader should here probably be warned that the following pages are to be looked at with a good deal of perception. As was pointed out earlier, there is an imaginative sense of seeing the frozen moment as part of an ever-moving, ever-changing current, but a certain amount of further imagination will be required when the reader realizes that we have not chosen to show the human animal as doing the movements of the ballet. Another creature, more naturally adapted to leaps and hops and stretches, will be cavorting, more or less successfully but with manifest sincerity, through the pages that follow. It is our hope that in addition to having been able, presumably, to shake off the shackles of the familiar, conventional and expected, the reader will also approach what is in store for him or her with the awareness that there may be as much of value to be gleaned from imperfection as from perfection, whether it is that of human dancers or, indeed, of frogs.

Frogs *and the* Ballet

For your enjoyment — and possible edification — here are a few typical ballet positions and movements. The first group consists of the five basic positions that form the foundation of all classical ballet dancing. The second depicts certain positions and steps performed at the *barre* and in the center by a single dancer. And the third group illustrates some *pas de deux* movements, those in which two dancers are involved.

Finally, since we have shown you a number of individual dancers in various poses, we present you with the entire Corps-de-Frog-Ballet on stage, in a moment from one of their more notable productions.

PART I

*Positions and Movements
of Individual Dancers*

The Five Basic Positions

The First Position

Note the elemental nature of the first position. To the uninitiated, the ballerina seems to be just standing there. But the *way* she is standing is not nearly so easy to achieve as it might appear. Every part of the body, from the head to the toes, every muscle, is carefully controlled, but the pose is, nonetheless, a relaxed one. Our ballerina's apparently artless posture is the result of a conscious effort, which has in time become second nature to her.

The stupid look is optional.

"The stupid look is optional."

The Second Position

This, the second of the five positions from which all classic ballet dancing derives, is much like the first, except that the feet are separated by about twelve inches. They are still turned outward in a straight line, a position that might be somewhat difficult to maintain in a high wind. Fortunately, ballet is usually performed indoors, where the danger of sudden gusts is generally quite minimal.

The *attitude* of the arms in this position, as well as in the third, fourth and fifth positions, can be varied somewhat, depending on which school of ballet one is following. The entire business of just where and how to hold the arms is the subject of *port de bras*, and there is no exclusively "right" way, although there are innumerable "wrong" ways.

"A position...difficult to maintain in a high wind."

[9   ]

The Third Position

The third position is unique in that, while both feet are still turned outward, the heel of the right foot is directly in front of the heel of the left. It requires a turning of both legs, and that includes thighs, knees, calves and ankles as well as feet. This position, needless to say, would present distinct problems to the ballerina if she possessed jumbo thighs or calves. Consequently, the aspiring young dancer would do well to avoid as much excessive rotundity as possible. Dancing is difficult enough, after all, without having to put up with more physical possessions than are strictly required, not that such endowments would necessarily always be inappropriate in certain situations other than ballet. It all depends, perhaps, on what one considers important.

"...avoid as much excessive rotundity as possible."

The Fourth Position

Now, the fourth position is a bit more complicated. The right foot, turned outward, is in front of the left foot, at a distance of some ten to twelve inches. The third, fourth and fifth positions, may, of course, be reversed; that is, the dancer may put the left foot forward rather than the right. In this drawing, the right foot is almost directly in front of the left, but this can be varied by moving the right foot to the side so that its heel is in line with the toes of the left foot. This is known as fourth position *ouvert*, or open. If that sounds complex and a bit awkward, remember that the important thing is to make it appear natural and relaxed, even though every natural instinct would seem to indicate that this is hardly a position that one would normally take while, say, conversing with friends.

Our ballerina here, by the way, should be briskly reprimanded for looking anywhere but to the front. It is possible, however, that she's had enough of the morning's practice and is anticipating a little lunch.

"...hardly a position that one would normally take while conversing with friends."

The Fifth Position

The fifth position is similar to the third, except that instead of the heels being together, the heel of the right foot is in front of the left toes. This pose, and the first four, for that matter, are distinct and emphatic suggestions that the concept of pigeon toes has no place in the vocabulary of the classic ballet. Any tendency toward such a concept is severely frowned upon.

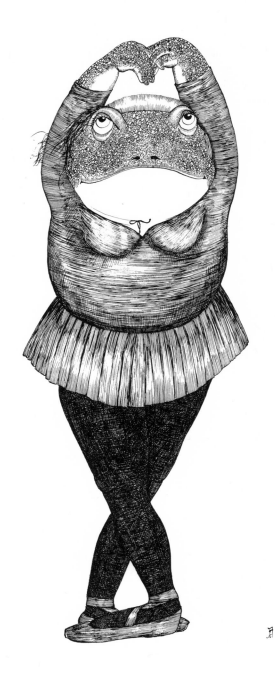

"The concept of pigeon toes has no place in the vocabulary of the classic ballet."

Some Positions and Steps
at the Barre and
at the Center

Pliés

A *plié* is, literally, a "fold" or "bend." In ballet, the term refers to a bending of the knees over the toes, and it is a movement inherent in almost all ballet steps. For this reason it is practiced diligently, if not doggedly, by both beginners and advanced dancers. If the feet are close together, as in the first position, the heels must, of course, rise from the floor as the *plié* is executed, but if the feet are farther apart, the entire foot remains flat on the floor throughout the movement.

In a *grand plié*, the body is lowered nearly as far as it will go, while in a *demi-plié*, the downward movement is stopped well before it has reached its limit. The *demi-plié* is often part of a more complex step and can be performed with one or both legs bent.

It is very easy to do a *plié* incorrectly. If the back does not remain straight, if the *derrière* protrudes beyond a certain acceptable degree, if the extreme position of the *plié* resembles that of an aborigine deep in a Sumatran jungle studying a tiger spoor, then suddenly and effortlessly the character of the *plié* has changed from grace to awkwardness, from expressiveness to absurdity. How easily that fine line is crossed, and how periously close to folly come the best efforts of men and frogs!

"[The plié*] is practiced diligently, if not doggedly . . ."*

Entrechat

This movement, performed here in the center, consists of a lively leap into the air, commencing from the fifth position, and a brisk beating together of the calves, in this case with the right leg behind the left. One of the difficulties of this particular movement is that upon alighting, the right leg must end up in *front* of the left. One too many beats and — since there is usually no way to lower the floor quickly — disaster is at hand.

Naturally, the more beats the dancer can perform the better, and some dancers have done as many as eight in one leap, but that is little short of phenomenal.

"One too many beats and...

Arrowood

disaster is at hand."

[21   ]

Grand Jeté

This, one of the most spectacular of ballet's movements, requires great elevation, a wide separation of the legs, and the semblance of effortless ease. It helps if the dancer can pause a moment at the top of his leap, but so far as is known, none has ever achieved anything but the *appearance* of a pause, although *that* is sometimes done so well that one might almost believe that the dancer has, finally, somehow managed to suspend the inexorable law of gravity.

"It helps if the dancer can pause a moment at the top of his leap."

[23   ]

Pas de Chat

Literally, a "leap of a cat," the *pas de chat* is a light and lithe spring into the air in which both feet come briefly together at the top of the leap. A catlike leap it assuredly is, and while its major feature lies in what happens while the dancer is in the air, it is no less important that he or she not alight on the floor with a thud. Cats never thud, and, of course, neither do frogs; even elephants seldom thud. It is human beings who thud, and although it is highly important in ballet that thuds be avoided, it is also possible that we should all make an earnest attempt to go through life with as little thudding as possible.

"...we should all...go through life with as little thudding as possible."

Cabriole

The *cabriole* may be executed forward or backward, to the right or left, and from various preparatory positions. It involves a leap into the air and a beating of the legs together while in the air. The original meaning of the French word *cabriole* is "caper," and the effect of the step is, indeed, that of a light, rather frolicsome little movement appropriate, perhaps, to a playful and merry moment in a ballet.

This may be a good time to mention that ballet positions and movements do not always in themselves express a specific and readily identifiable mood. Rather, it is the entire context of the dance which gives a particular meaning to a particular step. To a large degree, this is also true, of course, of words. Anyone conversant with the modern lexicon, for example, knows instantly that words such as "wild," "bad," "cool," "heavy," and a host of others are understandable only in context, a fact which may, incidentally, be an underlying reason for a good many "generation gap" problems.

"...a light, rather frolicsome little movement..."

Pas Ballonné

The *pas ballonné* may be executed in all directions, and may be performed repeatedly as a series of movements. It is an exceedingly graceful little step and consists of a kind of bouncing or hopping motion combined with a flicking movement of the leg.

The French word *ballon* means, as one might expect, "balloon," but its connotation in ballet has nothing whatever to do with the shape of balloons. The idea implied is, rather, that of a kind of momentary suspension in the air, and it is this illusion that distinguishes a ballet leap from that of a circus acrobat, whose primary endeavor is merely to leap as high and as far as he can. It is important in ballet, particularly in the *jetés*, that a dancer attain elevation, that is, height and distance. But without the element of *ballon*, that split-second breathless pause in mid-air that characterizes the leaps of a true dancer, the dance is little more than an exhibition of physical and acrobatic skill. It is not art, and it is most certainly very far from fine ballet.

"...an exceedingly graceful   little step..."

Attitude

There are a large number of variations of the basic position of the *attitude*, a pose on one leg in which the other is lifted, carried back and bent at the knee. This one is an *attitude croisée derrière*. The left leg, slightly bent, extends rearward while the dancer is on *pointes* or *demi-pointe*.

While most of the French terms used in the ballet give at least some indication of the character of the pose or movement they name, *attitude* seems to give no comparable hint as to its meaning. On the other hand, an attitude *is* the posture one assumes, the impression one gives. Perhaps, then, the *attitude* in ballet is intended primarily to convey a feeling, a certain attitude, in effect.

If our ballerina's *attitude* is a good one, graceful, light and expressive, can we assume that her attitude toward life is the same? Of course not, for she is expressing in the best way she knows what her *dance* means. It is probably most of the rest of us, the nondancers, who must keep a sharp eye on the much broader range of impressions which our attitudes are conveying.

"...the attitude...[conveys]

...a feeling, a certain attitude..."

Arabesque

The *arabesque* is, rather obviously, not a position that can be held for any prolonged period of time. Balanced on the tip of one foot, the ballerina gives her audience a momentary glimpse of the *arabesque,* and then she is gone. But the impression of an effortless grace, produced by the precisely controlled relationships of arms, hands, legs, body and head, remains like the pure clear sound of a single flute note, flashed across space in an instant.

Perhaps it is the memory of a beautiful moment that is as important as the moment itself. Who of us has not experienced the bittersweet recollection of a perfect moment and has not hungered to have it back? It will not return, but one always can — perhaps one always *should* — look eagerly for the next *arabesque.*

"...one always should...look eagerly for the next arabesque!"

Développé

A développé involves an unfolding of the leg, its extension to the side, front or rear from a bent position. It is subject to numerous variations, and it is often combined with other movements such as *battements,* or beating movements.

As in most ballet positions and movements, the matter of balance in the *développé* is of paramount importance. In practice, with the *barre* as an aid, balance is considerably easier to maintain, but in the center, with nothing to rely upon but oneself, the problem becomes extraordinarily more difficult. A slight misjudgment, a momentary inaccuracy, and balance is lost, but that is true, of course, of many things besides dance. It is clear from the position of our ballerina that her body is perfectly balanced and from the look on her face that her mind, too, is perfectly balanced. There may, however, be some indication that there might not be a tremendous amount to *be* balanced behind her lovely eyes, but what care we of that? If she is performing her *développé* with equilibrium and poise, why should we be concerned about what she is thinking, how she is thinking, or even *if* she is thinking?

"A slight misjudgment,
a momentary inaccuracy,   *and balance is lost..."*

[35   ]

Pas de Deux

Pirouette

The term *pirouette* — or "tour" — refers to multiple turns on one foot on one spot. Here, the male partner in this *pas de deux* is lightly supporting the ballerina as she is about to begin her *pirouette*. Clearly, he must know just when to let go as well as just when not to, since it is he who to a large extent controls the beginning and the ending of the *pirouette*, and he must avoid giving even the slightest impression that he is clutching his partner.

This movement is a somewhat dizzying one to watch. It is also probably a somewhat dizzying one to perform. Our ballerina does not always wear a crown while she performs the *pirouette*, but, for obvious reasons, when she does, she finds a suction cup arrangement to be a distinct convenience.

A perfectly executed *pirouette* is a thing of electrifying grace. No picture can do it justice, for its essence, like that of ballet itself, is movement.

. *its essence, like that of ballet itself, is movement.''*

Arabesque Penchée

Lightly supported by her partner, the ballerina dips into a leaning *arabesque*, a variation of the *arabesque* she performed earlier by herself. It is a fleeting pose that will quickly resolve itself into a different position, but for a moment it is a brilliant example of coordinated grace by both dancers.

The ideally coordinated actions of two dancers is, of course, central to any *pas de deux*, and the relationship of the performers is not unlike that of singer and accompanist. A flaw on the part of either partner can and usually will seriously diminish the stature of an entire performance. A mutual dependency and harmony must exist, and in the world of ballet a number of immensely successful partnerships have developed.

Would it be too fanciful to suggest that this essential of the *pas de deux* is a mirror of *any* successful partnership?

"A mutual dependency and harmony must exist..."

Grand Jeté

The literally supportive function of the male dancer in a *pas de deux* is nowhere better exemplified than in the spectacular *grand jeté*. It is a subtle support that the dancer gives his partner, for were he to become too obvious in his role, the entire effect of grace and ease would be destroyed. He must possess considerable strength in addition to poise, agility and a split-second sense of timing, and everything he does must appear to be perfectly natural and without strain.

Perhaps all our best efforts are somewhat like this. We usually know, after all, what we *should* do, that we probably *should* love and forgive, for example, but it is only when such things come naturally and spontaneously that they become really worthwhile and full of grace.

"It is a subtle support

that   the dancer gives his partner..."

[43   ]

Petit Battement

Many steps in ballet involve a kind of beating motion of the legs. At some times this is done in the air, at others, as in this example, with the dancer on *pointes*.

Our ballerina here is performing a *petit battement sur le cou-de-pied*, that is, with the left foot executing a beating movement alternately against the front and back of the right ankle. Although she is perfectly capable of doing this step alone, she is accepting the support of her partner because this is a *pas de deux* and she really hasn't much choice about the matter. On the other hand, it *is* somewhat reassuring for her to know that he is there not as a rival but as a complementary partner who may, if he performs well, make her dancing even more dazzling than it would be if she were alone.

à Edward Gorey

" . . . it is somewhat reassuring for her to know that he is there . . . "

Attitude

This *attitude* is basically the same position as that of the ballerina on page 31. But here she is performing her *attitude* as part of a *pas de deux*, and the overall effect of the pose is altered as a result. While the ballerina is the predominant figure, there is a unity, a kind of wholeness to the position that depends inescapably on both dancers. Taken separately, each is relaxed, graceful and in perfect control, but the relationship of one to the other is the added dimension which lends this, or any *pas de deux*, its unique oneness.

Edgar Allan Poe, in speaking of the short story, said that its most important element lay in what he called a "unity of impression," and there can be little question that he had, indeed, identified its essential characteristic. But he could as easily have been speaking of a *pas de deux* in ballet, and while his concern was specifically literary, the insight he expressed was one with a universal significance for all art.

" . . . a unity, a kind of wholeness . . . that depends inescapably on both dancers."

Pas Poisson

The remarkable *pas poisson* is a complex movement in which the ballerina plunges into a sort of "fish dive," curved around her partner's body and supported purely by her position relative to his and not by his hands. It is a position of virtuosity requiring great skill, and is not to be attempted by those who are still trying to get the hang of the first position.

In music and ballet, there is nearly always the necessity for some kind of logical and readily identifiable ending. In instrumental music, this is often accomplished by a coda, or formal concluding section; in a ballet *pas de deux*, the conclusion might be a *pas poisson*, a position the dancers hold as the music ends and the audience begins, presumably, to applaud.

It is good for things to be brought to an end. Some composers seem to have difficulties bringing their works to an end, some writers with concluding their stories. Some people don't know quite when to stop talking, and others experience excruciating problems in terminating visits. Perhaps this is because everyone has the instinctive feeling that an ending should somehow be logical, fitting and nonabrupt. At such moments one may envy the position of the dancers who perform the *pas poisson* as the curtain goes down.

"It is good for things to be brought to an end."

PART II

Corps-de-Frog-Ballet

The Final Bow
"Bravo"